WHEN THE SHADBUSH BLOOMS

BY Carla Messinger, WITH Susan Katz

ILLUSTRATED BY David Kanietakeron Fadden

TRICYCLE PRESS
BERKELEY | TORONTO

ABOUT THIS BOOK

It has been said that it's traditional to adapt, and that is what this book is about. We all learn from each other, and as we learn, we change. By the mid-1600s, when waves of white traders were traveling through Lenape land, we were trading furs for the European goods that soon became part of our lives. We saw ourselves decorating our clothing both with quillwork and also with cut-glass beads. We were collecting sap in one-piece baskets and boiling it into syrup in iron pots. We were wearing necklaces made of wampum and also bracelets made from brass.

Our story takes place both yesterday and today. It is told by Traditional Sister and Contemporary Sister, each from her own time.

To the children of the future, so they may see that the past and the present are one. —C.J.S.M. and S.K.

A special waníshi (thank you) to Beverly Slapin and Judy Dow.

To my grandparents, Ray and Christine Fadden, who selflessly shared their wisdom with seven generations by passing on their stories, customs, and traditional Mohawk values. —D.K.F.

Text copyright © 2007 by Carla Messinger and Susan Katz
Illustrations copyright © 2007 by
  David Kanietakeron Fadden

The publisher wishes to thank Judy Dow and Beverly Slapin and Oyate for their gracious assistance throughout this project.

Tricycle Press
an imprint of Ten Speed Press
PO Box 7123
Berkeley, California 94707
www.tricyclepress.com

Design by Kristine Brogno
Typeset in Weiss and Papyrus.
The illustrations in this book were rendered in acrylics.

Library of Congress Cataloging-in-Publication Data

Messinger, Carla.
When the shadbush blooms / by Carla Messinger, with Susan Katz ;
illustrated by David Kanietakeron Fadden.
p. cm.
Summary: A young Lenni Lenape Indian child describes her family's life through the seasons. Includes facts about the Lenni Lenape Indians.
ISBN-13: 978-1-58246-192-2
ISBN-10: 1-58246-192-9
1. Delaware Indians--Juvenile fiction. [1. Delaware Indians--Fiction. 2.Indians of North America--Middle Atlantic States--Fiction. 3. Seasons--Fiction. 4. Family life--Fiction.]
I. Katz, Susan. II. Fadden,
David Kanietakeron, ill. III. Title.
PZ7.M557Wh 2007
[E]--dc22
2006017389

First Tricycle Press printing, 2007
Printed in Singapore

1 2 3 4 5 6 — 11 10 09 08 07

My whole family lives close to the land—and to each other— through the cycle of the seasons.

My grandparents' grandparents walked beside the same stream where I walk with my brother, and we can see what they saw. Deer leap in the woods. Hawks fly in circles overhead. Frogs splash, and turtles sun themselves.

In early spring, when the shadbush blooms like a white lace veil, we go fishing. Dad smiles when my brother or I catch a shad.

We roast the fish, and everyone enjoys it, especially the dog.

When the deer shed their winter coats and geese honk on the pond, Dad and my brother clear the land for our garden. Mom and I sing as we plant the corn, and the baby coos, shaking her rattle.

When the berries ripen, dangling like tiny hearts, we go berry picking. My brother and I race to see who can pick the fastest. The baby tastes her first berries. Her smeared face makes me laugh.

When the air hums with the wings of bees, my brother and I chase the crows from our garden. Together we gather honey. My brother ducks when a bee buzzes too close. I lick from one finger a drop as sweet as summer.

When tall stalks rustle and the ears of corn have grown fat, we roast corn with our friends. While Grandma carefully takes her corn off the cob, I gobble mine fast. The baby plays with a new doll, and my brother scores a goal for his team.

When grasshoppers patter in the fields and the evenings echo with insect song, we enjoy the autumn harvest. Mom finds a pumpkin so big she can hardly carry it. Grandma shows the baby a beautiful gourd. My brother and I catch grasshoppers.

Sakaweuhewi Gischuch
Pooxit Gischuch

When the leaves fly like red and yellow wings, and nuts tumble from the trees, Dad makes the house snug and warm before cold weather. My brother and I rake a huge pile of leaves and jump in.

Deer Hair Turns Gray Moon
Falling Leaves Moon

When gray skies drop flakes that glitter like falling stars, my brother and I climb the hill. Grandpa gives us a push at the top, and we fly down. The dog races after us, barking.

When the days grow short, and trees creak and crack with the cold, Grandma mends our winter clothes and Grandpa tells us all stories. While we settle in, Mom fixes a snack. I ask to hear my favorite story twice.

Anixi Gischuch

When ground squirrels dig in the drifts of snow and birds perch on frozen branches, the boys start a snowball fight with the girls. Mom stocks the house with food. My brother and I remember to share with the animal people.

When spring peepers chirp their froggy songs,
we go on a trip with Grandma to gather maple
sap. The baby tastes her first spring treat.
I talk to a frog on a tree trunk.

As the seasons circle around once more, my brother and I walk to the stream. We watch for the shadbush to bloom again, as my grandparents' grandparents did.

ABOUT THE LENNI LENAPE

Before contact, our people, the Lenni Lenape—which means First, Real, or Original People—lived in a vast forest that covered parts of what are now called Pennsylvania, New York, New Jersey, Maryland, Delaware, and Connecticut. We were hunters, fishers, and farmers, and our villages were located along the banks or tributaries of a river that we called Lenape Wihittuck, "the river of the people." The Europeans renamed our river the "Delaware," in honor of Sir Thomas West III, or 12th Baron de la Warr, governor of Virginia. Because we lived along the river, they called us the "Delaware Indians."

Our people belonged to many clans, including Turkey, Turtle, Wolf, Deer, and Bear. Each of our villages was independent of the others, and our ways of living varied according to the climate and ecology of our particular location. But we were one people, all speaking dialects of a single language, part of the large Algonkian family of languages.

Our Lenape people were generous and welcomed the strangers to our homeland. By the mid-1600s, we were trading with the strangers. We gave them food, furs, and hides, and they gave us brass and iron pots, and metal knives and axes. But by the beginning of the 1700s, the abundant land that had fed us and taken care of us for centuries was suffering. While market hunters were killing off our game animals, farmers and lumbermen were clear-cutting our forests and damming, polluting, and over-fishing our rivers and streams. And eventually the settlers' encroachment made life impossible for us and forced most of us to migrate north to Canada or west to places from Ohio to Oklahoma. While some of us remained here, our lives were very difficult, and by the 1900s, we were "hiding in plain sight" and struggling to survive.

Only recently, in the late twentieth century, have we begun to reclaim our language and histories, our wisdom and knowledge. We are reclaiming our ceremonies and songs, our stories and art. We are reclaiming and cultivating our medicine plants. We are reclaiming our old ways of making and using flint, stone, bone, and wood tools. We are reclaiming our old ways of making beautiful deerskin clothing with naturally dyed quillwork. Although we work in the modern world as truck drivers, teachers, factory workers, and chiropractors, we are reclaiming how to live in the natural world. Look around. We are still here. We continue to practice our people's traditions and to follow the circle of the seasons.

ABOUT THE LENAPE SEASONS

Unlike the European calendar—which assigns a fixed number of days to each month—Sun, Moon, and the natural world have always guided our lives. For countless generations, we have followed the cycles of fishing, hunting, planting, tending gardens, and taking in the harvest. We named each cycle—each moon—for a significant aspect of nature, and each cycle brings its particular tasks and special pleasures.

MORE ABOUT
LENNI LENAPE CULTURE
TOLD BY TRADITIONAL SISTER

SIQUON (SEE' KON): "SPRING"

Mechoammowi Gischuch (mesh oh a mow' wee gee' shux*):
When the Shadfish Return Moon

When the shadfish return, we harvest leeks to eat with the cooked shad. After a long cold season, fresh new greens are important for our good health and well-being. The deer know this, too. When the shadbush blooms in the uplands, we move to the lowlands to fish for shad. Sometimes shad can grow as big as salmon, so we sometimes need help to bring in the catch.

Uskiquall awk Kaag'uk Gischuch (us kee' kal owk kax' ook gee' shux): **Grass and Geese Moon**

Ehackihewi Gischuch (ay hak ee hay' wee gee' shux): **Planting Moon**

Usually, men and boys clear the fields and women and girls plant the seeds. We all sing our thanksgiving to the seeds to help them grow.

W'tehimoewi Gischuch (wih tay hee mow ay' wee gee' shux): **Heartberry Moon**

Lenape land is blessed with many kinds of berries, each ripening in its own time. Shadberries and heartberries are the first. We enjoy their sweet taste and look forward to the others.

KITSCHINIPEN (KITSCH IN EE' PEN): "SUMMER"

Jagatamoewi Gischuch (yah gah tah mow ay' wee gee' shux): **Bees Moon**

Sometimes we get tired of chasing crows. That's when our grandparents keep us company and keep us alert to our responsibilities to the community.

Winaminge (win ah meeng' ay): **Moon of Roasting Ears of Corn**

We roast, grind, and parch flint corn, and also make it into cornmeal. We play ball games before the Thunderers come. The games are great fun and teach us skills that we need to hunt, fish, and do other things. At the end of the last ball game in kitschinipen, an elder woman rips open the ball and lets the deer hair fly free.

Kschichksowagon Gischuch (k'shish so wah' gahn gee' shux): **Grasshoppers Moon**

The grasshoppers crawl all over the grass. They are barely hopping because of the cooler nights. It's a game to catch and then release them. This is also the time to dry seeds for the next planting and to dry pumpkins.

*Note: "x" is pronounced as a gutteral "ch"

TACHQUOAK (TAX KO' AK): "AUTUMN"

Sakaweuhewi Gischuch (sah ka woy hay' wee gee' shux): Deer Hair Turns Gray Moon

Pooxit Gischuch (po o' xit gee' shux): Falling Leaves Moon

A wikwam is a small family lodge, and a longhouse shelters an extended family. We build them both with sapling poles that we bend and tie together, then put sheets of bark on top, and then bend and tie more sapling poles over the bark.

Winigischuch (wee nee gee' shux): Falling Snow Moon

We look forward to this time because of the many games we cannot play without the snow. To make a toboggan, we soak ash planks and mold them into shape. We braid deer hide to make the straps.

LOWAN (LOW' AN): "WINTER"

Mechakhokque (mesh ahx ho' kay): Cold Makes the Trees Crack Moon

Inside the wikwam, reed mats that we have woven hang on the walls and lay on the floor to help keep the lodge warm, and cedar boughs cover the ground for a fresh smell. There is a fire pit in the center of the wikwam for light, heat, and cooking, and a hole at the top to let the smoke out. We can change the direction of the smoke hole by rotating the flaps on top.

Anixi Gischuch (ah nee' xee gee' shux): Ground Squirrels Run Moon

After we finish with our snowball fight, we're pretty cold and wet, so it's good to go in and have hot stew: corn, beans, chunks of pumpkin, and deer meat all cooked together. Warm, filling, and delicious!

Tsquali Gischuch (t'skah' lee gee' shux): Frogs Begin to Croak Moon

We collect maple sap and boil it down into syrup to make maple sugar cakes. Originally, we collected sap in bark buckets and boiled it in wooden trenches, but now we use brass and iron pots, for which we trade from the Europeans.

Mechoammowi Gischuch (mesh oh a mow' wee gee' shux): When the Shadfish Return Moon

As Moon continues to circle around Earth, so does Lenape time.

Carla J.S. Messinger, Turtle Clan Lenape, was born in Allentown, Pennsylvania, where she still lives with her husband, Allan, and her librarian daughter, Joy. She spent childhood vacations on the old family farm in Bucks County, where she tended crops, milked the cows, and heard stories of the old ways from her grandparents and uncles. Carla says, "Once, when I caught a bad chest cold, I endured an old family remedy of skunk oil and goose grease rubbed onto a wet cloth that was wrapped around a heated flat stone and placed on my chest. It worked!" Carla is the founder and retired executive director of the Lenni Lenape Historical Society and Museum of Indian Culture. Currently the director of Native American Heritage Programs, she gives presentations about traditional Lenape lifeways and other Native American topics at schools, libraries, and elsewhere. *When the Shadbush Blooms* is Carla's first children's book. You can visit her website at www.lenape.info.

Susan Katz grew up in a small Pennsylvania Dutch town where she spent much of her childhood exploring—with her beagle friend, Joe—the meadows and woods Lenape children had explored thousands of years before. A poet from the time she was a teenager, Susan first began writing children's books when her son, Demian, at age two, decided to help her write. Sue says, "I was still writing with a typewriter back then, and what he really wanted was to bang on the keys. Finally, though, he actually dictated to me the first three sentences of a story. And then, being a two-year-old, he lost interest in it. But I didn't!" Susan's books for children include four poetry collections and a prizewinning novel, *Snowdrops for Cousin Ruth*. Demian is now grown, and Susan lives in Valley Forge, Pennsylvania, with her husband, David, and a house rabbit named Beauregard who considers himself the head of the family. You can visit her at www.netaxs.com/~katz.

David Kanietakeron Fadden, Wolf Clan Mohawk, was raised in Onchiota, New York, in a traditional Mohawk household. He was nurtured and taught by his father, John Kahionhes Fadden, educator, painter, and illustrator; his mother, Elizabeth Eva Karonhisake Fadden, wood sculptor and potter; and his paternal grandparents, Ray Tehanetorens Fadden, educator, naturalist, author, and founder of the Six Nations Indian Museum of Onchiota, and Christine Skawennati Fadden. David says, "At a very young age I would watch my father paint or draw and from time to time ask him questions about what he was painting. Inspired, I would use my crayons and draw on the walls of the house. My father then gave me a sketchpad and pencil. That's how I started." David's work has been featured in several exhibitions and can currently be seen at the Smithsonian Institution's National Museum of the American Indian in Washington D.C., and New York City. He has also contributed his art to a wide variety of books, periodicals, animations, and the television documentary "How the West Was Lost: Always the Enemy," broadcast on the Discovery Channel. He currently resides at the Mohawk Territory of Akwesasne, a community located on the Canadian-U.S. border, with his family, Margaret Kanatiiosta and her son Rarihwenhawi.